Jan. 28 2019 was my m̲i̲d̲d̲l̲e̲ day!

Dear Debby,

There are no words to express the thank
you that you rightfully deserve.
The kindness, care, devotion and warmth
that you have shown us, helped us get
through this challengin time.

G-d bless you and your Family!
Enjoy Out of Egypt !

With much gratitude,

David Moshe & Leah Moscowitz

We won't forget you, Thanks !

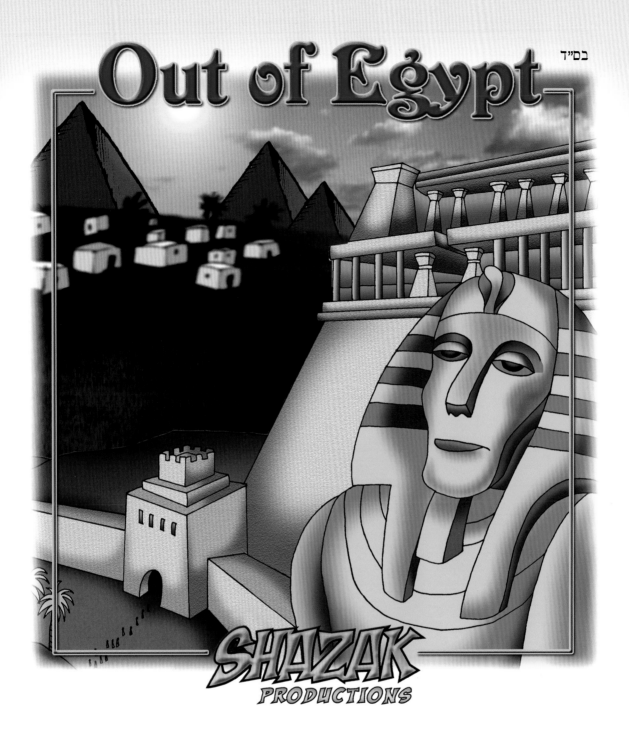

Out of Egypt

בס"ד

Distributed by Shazak Productions
www.shazak.com
mosheshazak@gmail.com
773.406.9880

Printed in China

Out of Egypt

An Illustrated Adaptation of the Book of Exodus

Script:
Rabbi Moshe Moscowitz
David Sokoloff

Artwork:
David Sokoloff
Jon Carter

Cover Design:
Devorah Haggar

SHAZAK
PRODUCTIONS

Table of Contents

Out of Egypt

is dedicated to the super *Shazak* staff (creators of *Queen of Persia, Miracle Lights* and *Out of Egypt* Books and Animated Cartoons):

David Sokoloff — Illustrator and Writer
John Napiorkowski — Cartoon Animator, Audio Editor
and Director
Jon Carter — Graphic Designer and Color Compositor
Michael Shoshani — Recording Engineer
Yael Resnick — Writer
Rabbi Zalman Kudan — Writer
Devorah Haggar — Graphic Designer
Leah Moscowitz — Consultant

Special Thanks to Rabbi Mendel Moscowitz, Rabbi Dovie Shapiro, Rabbi Yisroel Bernath, and Mr. Philip Weintraub for your insightful editing.

You have all used your amazing creative talents to educate and brighten the lives of countless people – young and old!

Rabbi Moshe Moscowitz
Executive Producer
Shazak Productions

Where Learning and Fun Meet!

Shazak Books and Animated Cartoons are highly recommended by Parents, esteemed Rabbis and Educators worldwide.
For Testimonials: Go to www.shazak.com

LONG, LONG AGO, THERE WAS A LAND OF VAST RICHES, KNOWN AS *EGYPT*. ITS MIGHTY KINGS, CALLED PHARAOHS, RULED WITH AN IRON FIST. WITH PYRAMIDS, PILLARS AND PALACES REACHING TO THE SKY, EGYPT WAS THE WONDER OF THE ANCIENT WORLD!

INTO THIS MAGNIFICENT EMPIRE CAME THE PEOPLE OF ISRAEL!

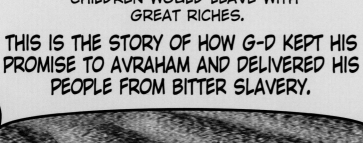

IT ALL BEGAN WHEN AVRAHAM, THE FATHER OF THE JEWISH NATION, EXPERIENCED AN AMAZING VISION.

IN HIS VISION, G-D PROMISED AVRAHAM THAT, ONE DAY, HIS CHILDREN WOULD HAVE A LAND OF THEIR OWN AND BECOME A LIGHT UNTO THE NATIONS.

BUT FIRST, THEY WOULD BE SLAVES FOR MANY YEARS IN A STRANGE LAND.

FINALLY, THEIR CRUEL SLAVE DRIVERS WOULD BE PUNISHED, AND AVRAHAM'S CHILDREN WOULD LEAVE WITH GREAT RICHES.

THIS IS THE STORY OF HOW G-D KEPT HIS PROMISE TO AVRAHAM AND DELIVERED HIS PEOPLE FROM BITTER SLAVERY.

ONLY 70 PEOPLE HAD COME DOWN WITH YAAKOV TO EGYPT, BUT THEIR NUMBER QUICKLY MULTIPLIED. SOON THE LAND WAS OVERFLOWING WITH THEM. AND NOT EVERYONE WAS HAPPY ABOUT THAT!

AND THEN...

A New King Arose in Egypt

RABBIS RAV AND SHMUEL DISAGREED OVER THE MEANING OF THE WORD "NEW":

I SAY, HE WAS A COMPLETELY NEW KING!

AND I SAY, THIS "NEW" KING WAS ACTUALLY THE SAME MAN, BUT FOR SOME REASON, HIS ATTITUDE HAD CHANGED.

HE NOW ACTED **AS IF** HE NEVER KNEW YOSEF!

EITHER WAY, HE WAS NO LONGER THE FRIENDLY PHARAOH OF YOSEF'S TIME.

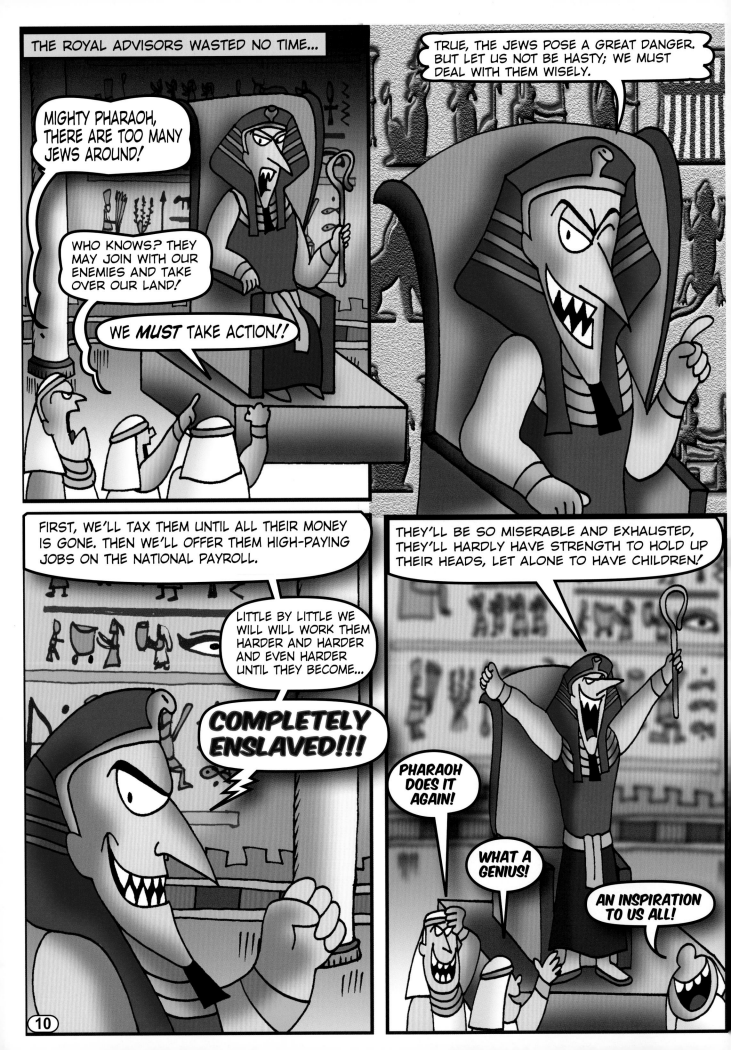

THEN THE EGYPTIANS RECRUITED A JEWISH POLICE FORCE.

LISTEN UP, POLICEMAN! IT'S YOUR JOB TO MAKE SURE YOUR GROUP OF SLAVES COMES UP WITH AT LEAST 6,000 BRICKS EVERY SINGLE DAY!

AND USE YOUR WHIPS!

WHIPS?!

OUCH!

OY VEY!

THAT HURTS!

BUT THE JEWISH POLICEMEN TREATED THEIR WORKERS KINDLY.

HAVE A REFRESHING DRINK, SHMUEL.

OKAY LEVI, THE COAST IS CLEAR. REST UP.

WHEW

YOUR WORKERS ARE SHORT 20 BRICKS!

TELL US WHO'S TO BLAME OR WE'LL WHIP YOU!

WE WILL NEVER INFORM ON OUR FELLOW JEWS.

GO AHEAD! WHIP ME!

Daily Hard Labor Report

Insights

YEARS LATER, G-D REWARDED THESE POLICEMEN.

WHEN MEMBERS OF THE GREAT SANHEDRIN, -THE HIGH COURT OF ISRAEL- WERE APPOINTED, MOSHE WAS INSTRUCTED TO CHOOSE THESE BRAVE POLICEMEN.

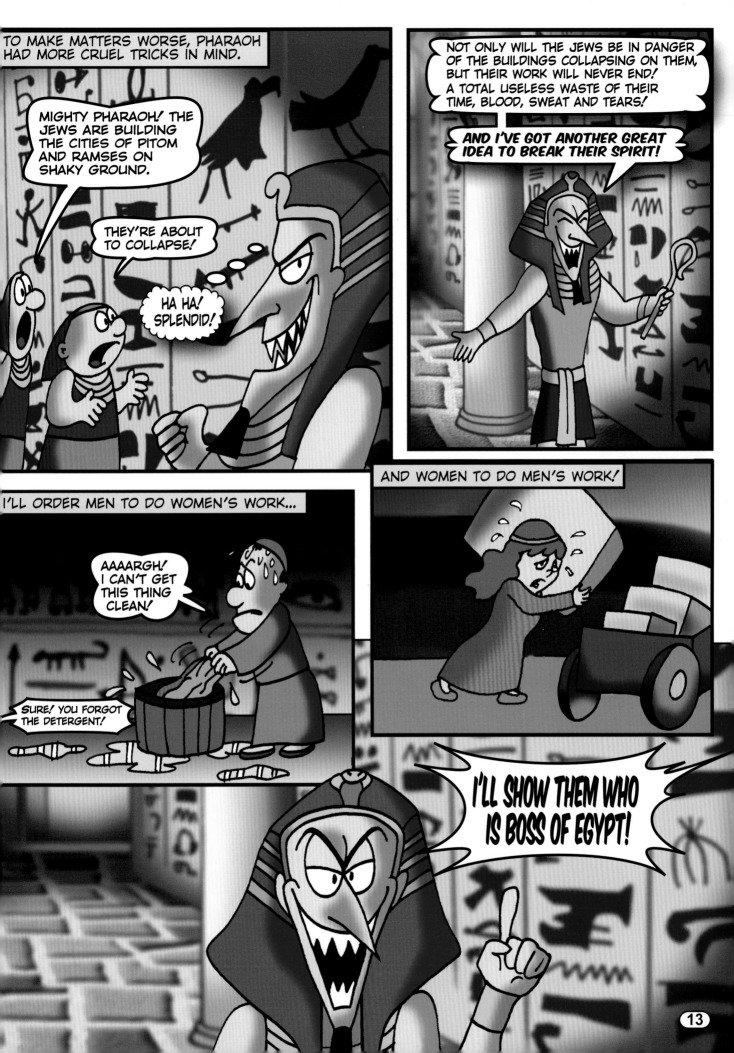

MOTHER, WHAT ARE WE TO DO? WE CAN'T POSSIBLY...

SHHH, PUAH.

OF COURSE, WE WILL NOT HARM THE BABIES. WE MUST WARN ALL MOTHERS TO HIDE THEIR NEWBORNS.

NOT ONLY THAT, WE'LL PROVIDE THEM WITH PLENTY OF FOOD AND DRINK!

WITH THE HELP OF THE ALMIGHTY, WE **WILL** SAVE THE BABIES FROM THE WICKED PHARAOH.

WATER

FOOD

LATER...

SHIFRAH & PUAH MIDWIVES
1.800.CALLNOW
We Care

Shazak

PHARAOH COMMANDS SHIFRAH AND PUAH TO REPORT IMMEDIATELY!

DON'T WORRY, DEAR. I HAVE AN IDEA.

WHAT'RE YOU GOING TO SAY, MOTHER?

THE BASKET WITH THE LITTLE BABY SAILED GENTLY DOWN THE NILE RIVER UNDER MIRIAM'S WATCHFUL EYES.

25

HE WAS TALLER THAN OTHER CHILDREN HIS AGE, AND STEADILY GREW STRONGER, WISER, AND MORE HANDSOME.

COME HERE, MY DEAR SON.

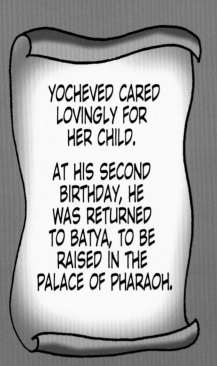

YOCHEVED CARED LOVINGLY FOR HER CHILD.

AT HIS SECOND BIRTHDAY, HE WAS RETURNED TO BATYA, TO BE RAISED IN THE PALACE OF PHARAOH.

BATYA HAD LEARNED THE HEBREW LANGUAGE AND WITH THE HELP OF HEAVENLY INSPIRATION...

I'VE DECIDED UPON A HEBREW NAME FOR YOU.

SINCE YOU WERE DRAWN FROM THE WATER, I WILL CALL YOU

MOSHE,

FOR THAT IS WHAT THE NAME MEANS IN HEBREW.

AND I'LL CALL YOU MOM.

Insights

MOSHE HAD NINE OTHER NAMES, INCLUDING AVIGDOR, YEKUTIEL, AND TUVYA. YET THE TORAH ALWAYS CALLS HIM MOSHE, THE NAME BATYA GAVE HIM.

G-D SAID, "SINCE *YOU* ARE THE ONE WHO SAVED THE BOY'S LIFE, I WILL CALL HIM BY THE NAME *YOU* GAVE HIM!"

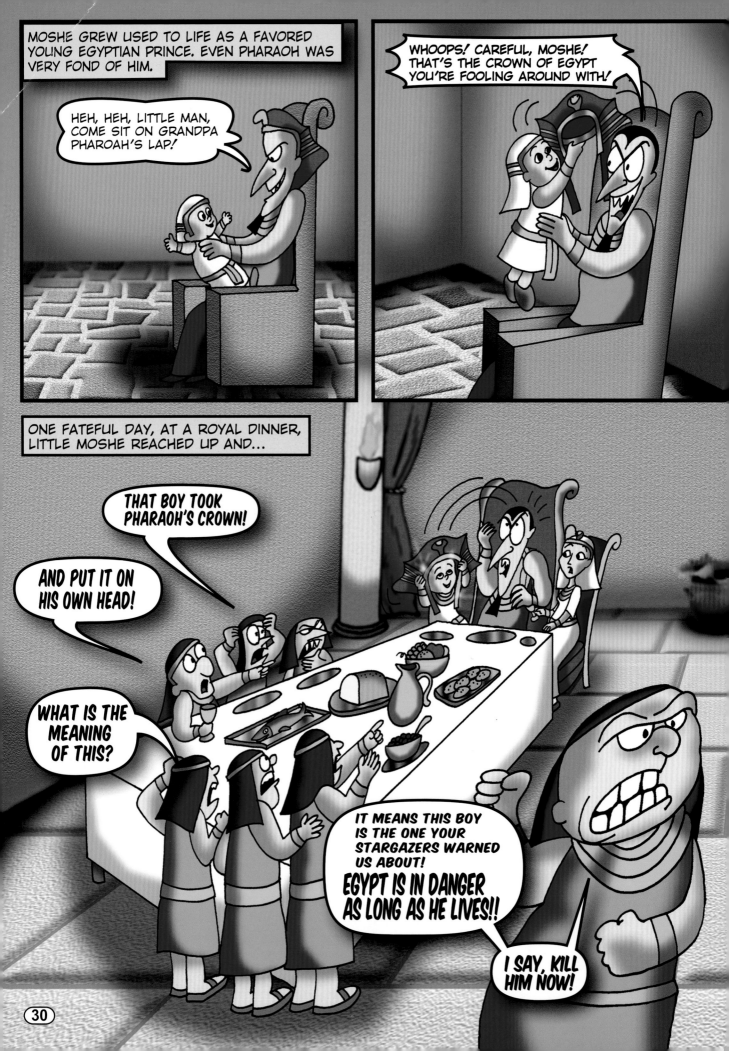

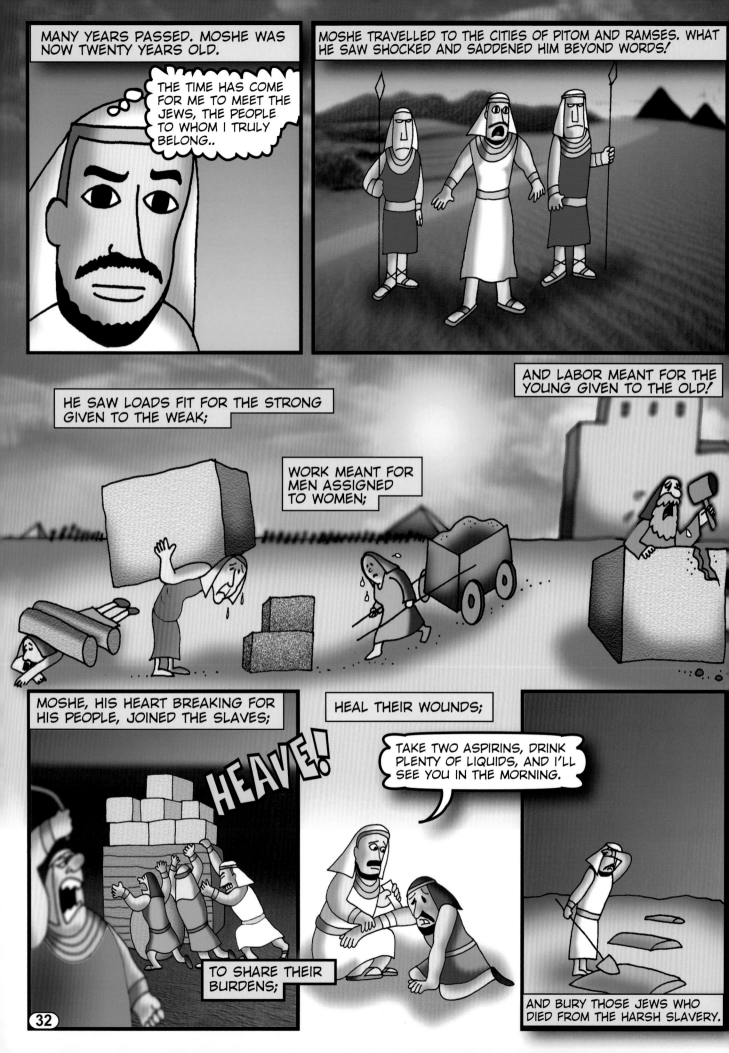

DATAN AND AVIRAM WASTED NO TIME.

HE'S A VICIOUS MURDERER!

VERY DANGEROUS!

OFF WITH HIS HEAD!

HOLD STILL, MOSHE. YOUR TROUBLES WILL SOON BE OVER!

HA HA HA
chuckle chuckle
snicker snicker
Hardy Har Har Har!!

A MIRACLE HAPPENED: MOSHE'S NECK BECAME SOLID MARBLE!

CLANG!

AS MOSHE FLED THE PALACE. PHARAOH SENT SOLDIERS IN HOT PURSUIT, BUT THEY WERE MIRACULOUSLY STRUCK BLIND!

STOP, MOSHE!

WHEREVER YOU ARE!

AFTER MANY, MANY, YEARS OF ADVENTURES, MOSHE, WHO WAS NOW 67 YEARS OLD, MOVED TO THE LAND OF MIDYAN.

MOSHE CHOSE TO LIVE NEAR A WELL, BECAUSE HIS ANCESTORS, YITZCHAK AND YAAKOV, FOUND THEIR WIVES BY A WELL.

AT THAT TIME, THE PRIEST OF MIDYAN WAS YITRO. IN SPITE OF THE HONOR AND RICHES HEAPED UPON HIM, YITRO WAS DEEPLY UNHAPPY.

HMMPH! I HAVE TO APPEAR TO WORSHIP ALL THESE FOOLISH IDOLS BECAUSE THE PEOPLE EXPECT IT OF ME.

IN TRUTH, I AM LIVING A LIE!

THESE SENSELESS BLOCKS OF WOOD AND STONE HAVE EYES BUT CANNOT SEE, EARS BUT CANNOT HEAR, AND MOUTHS THAT CANNOT TALK!

WHAT NONSENSE!

I MUST FIND THE TRUE GOD OF THE WORLD.

IT WAS A BRAVE DECISION, ONE THAT WOULD COST YITRO DEARLY.

FOR REJECTING THE ACCEPTED WORSHIP OF HIS COUNTRYMEN, WE HEREBY REJECT YITRO!

YEAH! LET NO ONE SPEAK TO HIM - EVER!

OR DO BUSINESS WITH HIM!

OR MARRY ANY OF HIS DAUGHTERS!

SINCE YITRO LOST ALL HIS HIRED HELP AND HAD NO SONS, HE HAD NO CHOICE BUT TO SWALLOW HIS PRIDE AND SEND HIS SEVEN DAUGHTERS TO TAKE CARE OF HIS SHEEP.

UDDENLY MOSHE APPEARED...

ONE DAY AT THE WELL...

WELL, WELL, WELL... LOOK, YOU GUYS! YITRO'S DAUGHTERS!

LET'S GIVE 'EM A HARD TIME!

HEY, YOU! OUTTA DA WAY! MEN FIRST!

HUH?

SURE, MISTER. WHATEVER YOU SAY.

STAY COOL! WE WAS JUST LEAVIN', Y' KNOW.

LEAVE THOSE LADIES ALONE!

HOW CAN WE EVER THANK YOU?

LET ME HELP YOU LADIES WATER YOUR FLOCK OF SHEEP.

THAT'S SO VERY KIND OF YOU!

GASP! THE WATER IS RISING UP TO HIM!

INCREDIBLE!!

SPLOOSH!

HUH?

IN TIME, MOSHE MARRIED YITRO'S DAUGHTER, THE BEAUTIFUL TZIPPORAH.

YITRO WAS DELIGHTED WITH HIS NEW SON-IN-LAW. HE GREATLY ADMIRED MOSHE AND TREATED HIM WITH THE UTMOST RESPECT.

Y'KNOW, MOSHE, I'VE ALWAYS WANTED A SON!

ONE DAY...

MOSHE! COME QUICKLY!

WHAT IS IT, TZIPPORAH?

WAAAAH!

WE HAVE A BABY BOY!

MAZAL TOV!!

LET'S CALL HIM GERSHOM, WHICH MEANS, "A STRANGER THERE."

THIS IS HOW WE WILL THANK G-D FOR LEADING ME TO MIDYAN. I CAME AS A STRANGER AND FOUND A HOME, WIFE AND FAMILY.

FAR FROM THE CLUTCHES OF PHARAOH!

MOSHE LIVED HAPPILY WITH HIS WIFE AND SON, AND TENDED YITRO'S SHEEP.

BUT THE TIME WAS FAST APPROACHING WHEN G-D WOULD ASK HIM TO LEAD ANOTHER FLOCK, ON A JOURNEY OUT OF EGYPT!

MOO?

BAAA BAAA

BAAA BAAA BAAA

BAAA x 4

MOO

MOSHE, YOU ARE LEADING THE FLOCK TOWARD THE WILDERNESS?!

YES; THAT IS THE ONLY WAY I CAN BE SURE THE SHEEP DON'T GRAZE ON PRIVATE PROPERTY.

BAAA x 5

TWEET

BAAA BAAA

BAAA

BAAA BAAA BAAA

BAAA BAAA BAAA

BAAA BAAA DITTO

I MUST SAY, TZIPPORAH, THAT HUSBAND OF YOURS IS REALLY SPECIAL!

UNDER HIS CARE, NOT ONE SHEEP HAS EVER BEEN LOST, OR HURT BY WILD BEASTS.

THE FLOCK IS GROWING BEYOND MY WILDEST DREAMS!

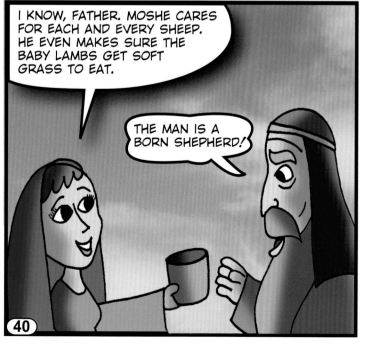

I KNOW, FATHER. MOSHE CARES FOR EACH AND EVERY SHEEP. HE EVEN MAKES SURE THE BABY LAMBS GET SOFT GRASS TO EAT.

THE MAN IS A BORN SHEPHERD!

AND I HAVE A FEELING THAT A GREATER FLOCK AWAITS HIM.

AND NOT JUST SHEEP!

WHAT IS THAT IN YOUR HAND?

A STAFF.

THROW IT TO THE GROUND.

GASP!

IT'S... A SNAKE!

I MUST RUN FOR MY LIFE!

DON'T GO AWAY, MOSHE... GRAB IT BY ITS TAIL.

IT'S BECOME A STAFF AGA[IN]

LET THIS BE THE FIRST SIGN.

NOW, PUT YOUR HAND BY YOUR CHEST AND THEN TAKE IT OUT.

MY HAND! IT'S WHITE LIKE SNOW... WITH LEPROSY!

PUT YOUR HAND BACK AND TAKE IT OUT ONCE MORE.

IT'S HEALED!

LET THAT BE THE SECOND SIGN.

HERE IS YET A THIRD SIGN...

TAKE SOME WATER FROM THE RIVER. WHEN YOU POUR IT UPON THE DRY LAND, IT WILL TURN TO BLOOD.

YOU WILL PERFORM THESE THREE SIGNS BEFORE THE ELDERS OF THE JEWISH PEOPLE AND THEY WILL BELIEVE.

MOSHE WAS STILL NOT READY TO ACCEPT HIS MISSION.

B...BUT... S... STILL... I... I AM NOT A MAN OF WORDS. I... I... STU... STUTTER!

WHO MAKES A MAN'S MOUTH? WHO GIVES HIM SPEECH?

IS IT NOT I, G-D?!

I BEG YOU, ALMIGHTY! DO NOT SEND ME!

Insights

WHY DIDN'T G-D SIMPLY CURE MOSHE OF HIS SPEECH PROBLEM?

G-D WANTED EVERYONE TO KNOW THAT IT WAS NOT BY MOSHE'S PERSUASIVE SPEECH THAT THE JEWS WERE FREED, BUT RATHER BY DIVINE POWER.

HAVE NO FEAR, MOSHE...
AHARON WILL BE YOUR SPOKESMAN.

WELL, NOW I CERTAINLY FEEL BETTER KNOWING THAT MY BROTHER AHARON ALSO HAS AN IMPORTANT POSITION. I WOULDN'T WANT AHARON TO FEEL BAD THAT G-D CHOSE ME OVER HIM.

NOW, TAKE YOUR STAFF AND LEAD MY PEOPLE... OUT OF EGYPT!

WITH TZIPPORAH AND THEIR TWO SONS, GERSHOM AND NEWBORN ELIEZER, MOSHE SET OUT FOR EGYPT.

AS THEY ENTERED EGYPT...

WHO COULD IT BE, MOSHE?

FATHER, LOOK! SOMEONE'S COMING!

GASP!

IT LOOKS LIKE ONE OF MY BRETHREN!

THE TWO BROTHERS WERE FINALLY REUNITED.

AHARON!

MOSHE!

AHARON, MY DEAR BROTHER!

MOSHE, WHERE HAVE YOU BEEN ALL THESE YEARS?

IN MIDYAN.

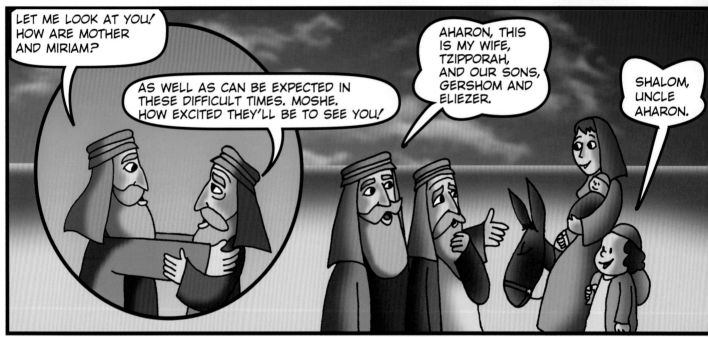

LET ME LOOK AT YOU! HOW ARE MOTHER AND MIRIAM?

AS WELL AS CAN BE EXPECTED IN THESE DIFFICULT TIMES. MOSHE. HOW EXCITED THEY'LL BE TO SEE YOU!

AHARON, THIS IS MY WIFE, TZIPPORAH, AND OUR SONS, GERSHOM AND ELIEZER.

SHALOM, UNCLE AHARON.

MOSHE, THERE'S ENOUGH JEWISH SUFFERING IN EGYPT. TAKE MY ADVICE: HAVE MERCY ON YOUR FAMILY AND SEND THEM BACK TO MIDYAN.

I SEE WHAT YOU MEAN.

TZIPPORAH, IT'S MUCH TOO DANGEROUS HERE IN EGYPT. TAKE THE BOYS BACK TO MIDYAN. MAY IT BE HEAVEN'S WILL THAT WE BE REUNITED SOON.

AW, I NEVER GET TO GO ANY-WHERE!

48

IMMEDIATELY UPON THEIR RETURN TO EGYPT, MOSHE AND AHARON GATHERED THE ELDERS OF THE JEWISH PEOPLE.

THE G-D OF OUR FATHERS, HAS APPOINTED MOSHE AS HIS MESSENGER TO PHARAOH...

BEARING HEAVEN'S COMMAND TO LET HIS NATION *OUT OF EGYPT!*

MOSHE SHOWED THE THREE SIGNS BEFORE THE ELDERS.

THE STAFF... A SNAKE!

GASP!

?!

YOUR HAND IS AS WHITE AS SNOW!

AMAZING!

THE WATER BECAME BLOOD!!

REDEMPTION IS NEAR!

PRAISE G-D!

FULL OF CONFIDENCE, THE ELDERS, LED BY MOSHE AND AHARON, MARCHED OFF TO THE ROYAL PALACE.

MIGHTY, GRACIOUS PHAROAH! HOW CAN THE WORKERS COME UP WITH THE SAME AMOUNT OF BRICKS WITHOUT ANY STRAW?

CAN WE *PLEASE* HAVE STRAW?

IN RESPONSE TO THIS REASONABLE REQUEST, PHARAOH DISPLAYS HIS USUAL "COMPASSION."

NOT A CHANCE!

THE FRUSTRATED JEWS CAME RUNNING TO MOSHE AND AHARON...

THIS YOU CALL REDEMPTION?!

IT'S NEVER BEEN THIS BAD!

GO BACK TO MIDYAN!

IN DESPERATION, MOSHE CRIED OUT...

ALMIGHTY G-D!

WHY HAVE YOU DONE EVIL TO THIS PEOPLE?!

SINCE I HAVE COME BEFORE PHARAOH THINGS HAVE GOTTEN WORSE!

53

MOSHE:
COMMAND THE KING OF EGYPT
TO LET MY PEOPLE GO.
I WILL SHOW THEM...

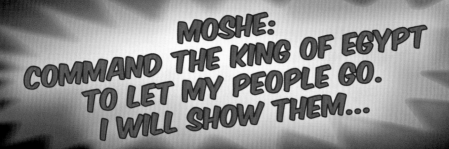

SIGNS AND WONDERS!

AHARON, G-D TOLD ME THAT A STORM OF PLAGUES WILL FALL UPON EGYPT SUCH AS THE WORLD HAS NEVER SEEN BEFORE!

FOR AN ENTIRE YEAR, AMAZING AND TERRIFYING EVENTS WILL PUNISH THE CRUEL EGYPTIANS.

FINALLY, IN THE MONTH OF NISSAN, PHARAOH WILL SET OUR PEOPLE FREE.

THE TWO ELDERLY BUT FEARLESS BROTHERS MARCHED FORWARD TO FACE PHARAOH.

AHARON WAS 83 YEARS OLD AND MOSHE WAS 80.

AT THE PALACE...

WHAT?! YOU'RE BACK?!

WE ARE MESSENGERS OF THE G-D OF ISRAEL.

G-D DEMANDS THAT YOU LET THE JEWISH PEOPLE *OUT OF EGYPT!*

DIVINE MESSENGERS, EH? *PROVE IT!*

AHARON, THROW DOWN YOUR STAFF.

AS SOON AS AHARON'S STAFF HIT THE GROUND, IT MIRACULOUSLY TURNED INTO A SNAKE!

56

Insights

THE LONGEST RIVER IN THE WORLD IS THE GREAT NILE RIVER (4,145 MILES LONG; LONGER THAN THE AMAZON RIVER!). SINCE IT HARDLY RAINED IN EGYPT, THE RIVER WAS CRUCIAL TO EGYPT'S SURVIVAL AND THEREFORE WORSHIPPED AS A GOD. FOR THAT REASON THE NILE WAS STRICKEN FIRST; TO PROVE TO ALL THAT THE G-D OF ISRAEL IS THE SUPREME POWER.

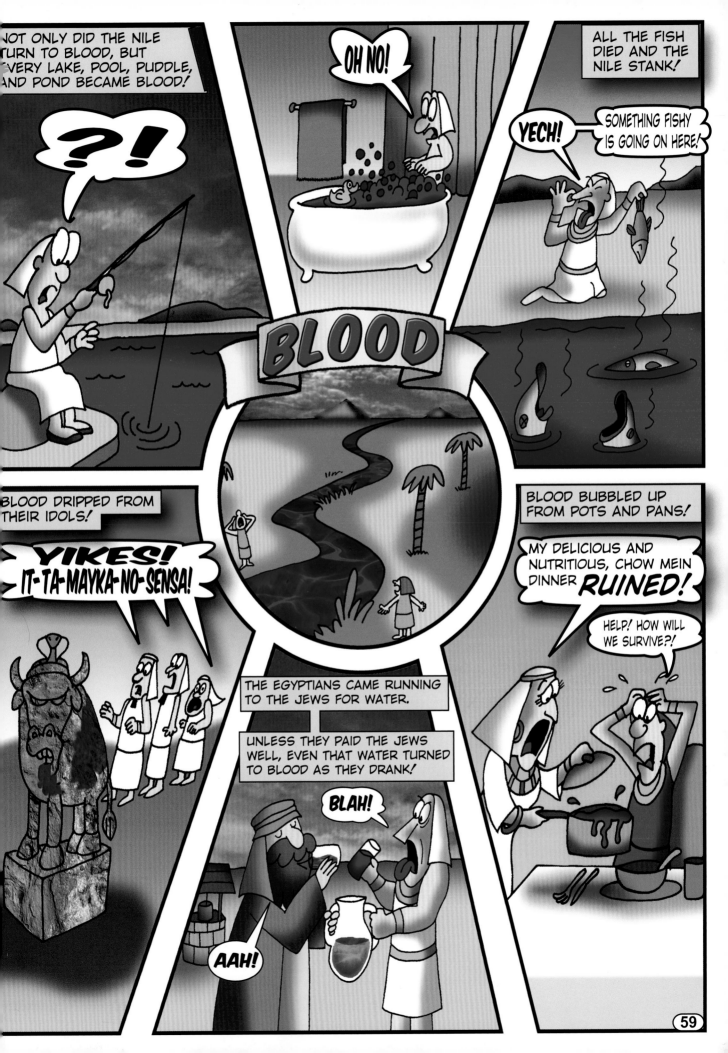

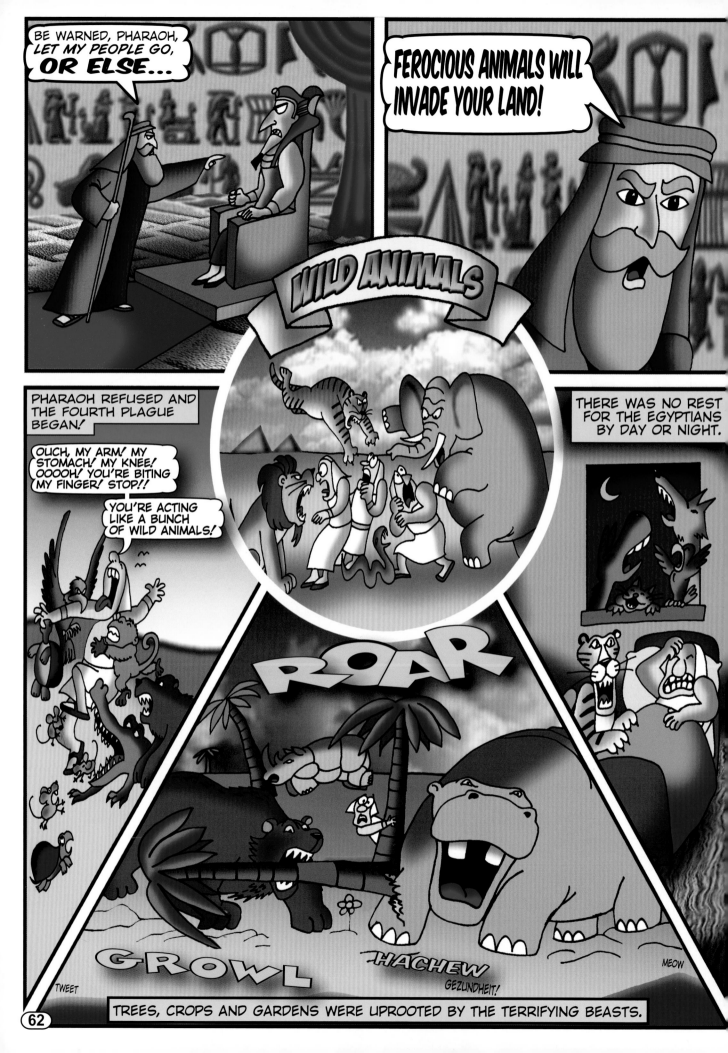

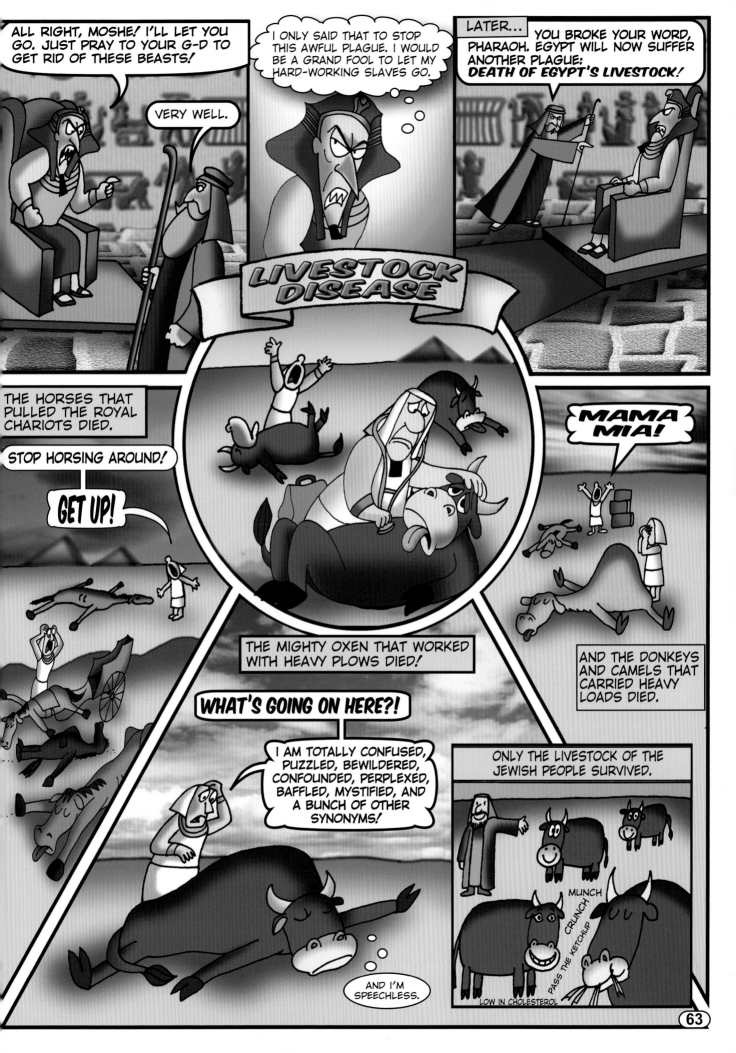

G-D COMMANDED MOSHE TO STRETCH OUT HIS HAND TO THE SKY, BRINGING A THICK BLANKET OF DARKNESS TO COVER ALL OF EGYPT - EXCEPT WHERE THE JEWS LIVED!

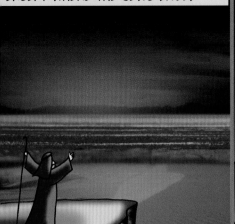

MY FELLOW JEWS:

BEFORE WE LEAVE THE COUNTRY, THE EGYPTIANS WILL OFFER US THEIR TREASURES.

DURING THESE DAYS OF DARKNESS, FIND OUT WHERE THESE VALUABLES ARE KEPT!

LIGHT FOLLOWED THE JEWS INTO THE HOMES OF THE EGYPTIANS.

NOW WE KNOW WHERE THEY HIDE THEIR TREASURES.

AND IF THEY CLAIM THEY HAVE NONE, WE CAN REMIND THEM.

FOR THE FIRST THREE DAYS, THE EGYPTIANS WERE PLUNGED INTO DARKNESS.

DARKNESS

THE NEXT THREE DAYS, THE DARKNESS BECAME SO THICK THAT THE EGYPTIANS WERE STUCK IN THEIR PLACES!

TURN ON THE LIGHTS! SOMEBODY... ANYBODY!

IS THIS SOME KIND OF A POWER OUTAGE?

DURING THIS PLAGUE, THE JEWS WHO FELT COMFORTABLE IN EGYPT AND WANTED NO PART OF G-D'S PROMISE OF FREEDOM, DIED AND WERE BURIED.

IT WAS TOO DARK FOR THE EGYPTIANS TO WITNESS THEIR DEATHS.

GO! GO! TAKE YOUR FAMILIES AND GO WORSHIP! JUST LEAVE YOUR ANIMALS.

ACTUALLY PHARAOH, WE'LL TAKE OUR ANIMALS *AND* YOURS!

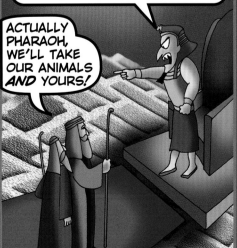

WHAT NERVE! NOW, I WON'T LET *ANY* OF YOU GO!

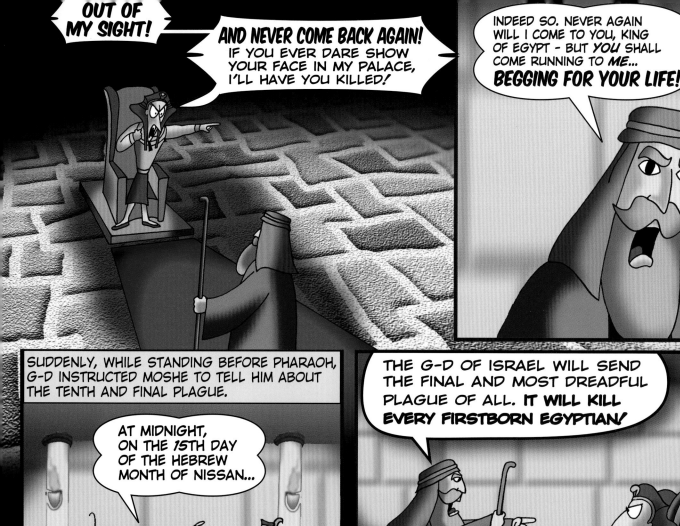

OUT OF MY SIGHT!

AND NEVER COME BACK AGAIN! IF YOU EVER DARE SHOW YOUR FACE IN MY PALACE, I'LL HAVE YOU KILLED!

INDEED SO. NEVER AGAIN WILL I COME TO YOU, KING OF EGYPT - BUT *YOU* SHALL COME RUNNING TO *ME*... BEGGING FOR YOUR LIFE!

SUDDENLY, WHILE STANDING BEFORE PHARAOH, G-D INSTRUCTED MOSHE TO TELL HIM ABOUT THE TENTH AND FINAL PLAGUE.

AT MIDNIGHT, ON THE *15TH* DAY OF THE HEBREW MONTH OF NISSAN...

THE G-D OF ISRAEL WILL SEND THE FINAL AND MOST DREADFUL PLAGUE OF ALL. **IT WILL KILL EVERY FIRSTBORN EGYPTIAN!**

THERE WILL BE A TERRIFYING OUTCRY IN THE LAND... CRIES OF PAIN, LOUDER THAN ANYTHING YOU'VE EVER HEARD OR WILL HEAR AGAIN!

THE NERVE OF PHARAOH TELLING ME NEVER TO COME BACK!

WITH FREEDOM ONLY DAYS AWAY, MOSHE SPOKE TO HIS PEOPLE.

MESSAGE FROM G-D!

THE TIME HAS COME TO PREPARE A SPECIAL OFFERING - THE *KORBAN PESACH* (PASSOVER SACRIFICE).

ON THE TENTH DAY OF THE MONTH OF NISSAN, LET EVERY FAMILY TAKE A LAMB. KEEP IT IN YOUR HOMES FOR FOUR DAYS.

MOSHE CONTINUED HIS INSTRUCTIONS...

"THEN, ON THE *14TH* OF NISSAN, THE LAMB SHALL BE SLAUGHTERED AND ROASTED WHOLE."

"AFTER NIGHTFALL EAT THIS LAMB QUICKLY, TOGETHER WITH *MATZAH* AND *MAROR* (BITTER HERBS)."

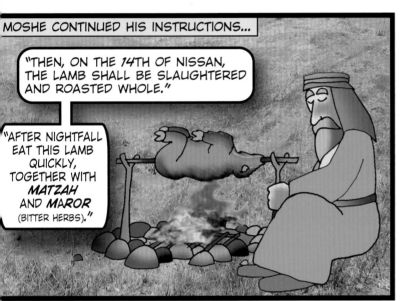

"TAKE SOME BLOOD OF THE SACRIFICE AND SMEAR IT ON THE TWO DOORPOSTS AND BEAM ABOVE THE DOORWAY."

GREAT PAINT JOB, DAD!

"WHEN THE LAST PLAGUE FALLS UPON EGYPT, KILLING ALL FIRSTBORN IN THE LAND, G-D WILL SEE OUR DOORPOSTS AND **PASS OVER** OUR HOMES, LEAVING US SAFE FOR THE GREAT EXODUS... **OUT OF EGYPT.**"

tick
tock
tick
tock

ON THE TENTH DAY OF NISSAN, A SHABBAT DAY TO BECOME FAMOUS IN YEARS TO COME...

DID YOU HEAR SOMETHING?

SOUNDS LIKE - A LAMB!

FELLOW EGYPTIANS: OUR GODS NEED OUR HELP!

EMERGENCY!

FOLLOW ME!

HURRY!

CALL 9-1-1!

HATZALAH!

OH, MY GOD!!

WHAT DO YOU THINK YOU ARE DOING?!

WE'RE NOT AFRAID OF YOU OR YOUR IDOLS! WE'RE PREPARING THIS LAMB FOR A SPECIAL PASSOVER OFFERING, CALLED KORBAN PESACH.

SOON, THE G-D OF ISRAEL WILL STRIKE DEAD ALL THE FIRSTBORN IN EGYPT, BUT WILL PASS OVER OUR HOMES.

BAAAAAA

THE EGYPTIANS WERE TERRIFIED!

COULD THIS BE TRUE?

WELL, DID YOU FORGET THE FIRST NINE PLAGUES?

WHATEVER MOSHE SAYS COMES TRUE!

71

WHEN THE EGYPTIAN FIRSTBORNS HEARD THIS, THEY FRANTICALLY RAN TO THEIR FATHERS.

THE NEXT PLAGUE MOSHE IS PREDICTING IS *THE-PLAGUE-OF THE-FIRSTBORN!*

DAD, HELP! SAVE US! CONVINCE PHARAOH TO LET THE JEWS GO!

WHAT?! ARE YOU OUT OF YOUR MINDS? GO TO PHARAOH?!

WHO KNOWS WHAT HE WILL DO TO US? **FORGET IT!**

YEAH! HOW ABOUT IF *YOU BOYS* GO TO PHARAOH?

THE FIRSTBORNS DID GO TO PHARAOH. HIS RESPONSE WAS SWIFT AND PREDICTABLE.

NO!!!
ABSOLUTELY NOT! AND GET OUT!

AND SO, RISING UP FROM FEAR AND FRUSTRATION, THE REVOLT OF THE FIRSTBORN SWEPT OVER EGYPT.

THE FIRSTBORN TOOK MATTERS INTO THEIR OWN HANDS.

HEY, WATCH OUT! THAT THING'S SHARP!

GOOD POIN

BLOODY CIVIL WAR BROKE OUT ALL OVER EGYPT. THOUSANDS OF FATHERS WERE KILLED BY THEIR FIRSTBORN CHILDREN.

Insights

ON THE TENTH DAY OF THE MONTH OF NISSAN, A SHABBAT DAY, THE EGYPTIANS FOUGHT AMONG THEMSELVES, LEAVING THE JEWS IN PEACE.

IT WAS TRULY AN AMAZING MIRACLE!

TO COMMEMORATE THIS EVENT, THE SHABBAT BEFORE PASSOVER WOULD FOREVER BE KNOWN AS *SHABBAT HAGADOL* (THE GREAT SHABBAT).

ON THE *14TH OF NISSAN*, THE JEWS CAREFULLY PREPARED THE *KORBON PESACH*.

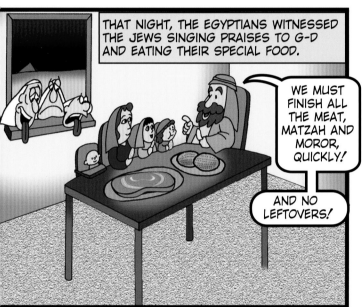

THAT NIGHT, THE EGYPTIANS WITNESSED THE JEWS SINGING PRAISES TO G-D AND EATING THEIR SPECIAL FOOD.

WE MUST FINISH ALL THE MEAT, MATZAH AND MOROR, QUICKLY!

AND NO LEFTOVERS!

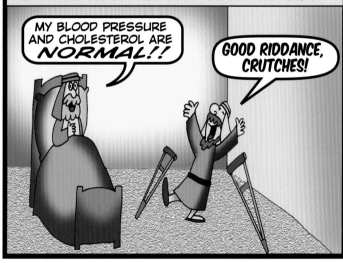

JEWS WHO WERE SICK MIRACULOUSLY RECOVERED! THIS WAS SO THE EGYPTIANS COULD NOT CLAIM THAT THE COMING PLAGUE HAD ALSO STRUCK THE JEWS.

MY BLOOD PRESSURE AND CHOLESTEROL ARE *NORMAL!!*

GOOD RIDDANCE, CRUTCHES!

PLEASE DO NOT DISTURB

Insights

NOTICE THAT THE BLOOD ON THE DOORFRAME FORMS THE SHAPE OF THE HEBREW LETTER *CHET*, WHICH IS THE FIRST LETTER OF *CHAIM*, THE HEBREW WORD FOR 'LIFE'.

ח = חיים

DURING THE PLAGUE OF THE FIRSTBORN, HOMES MARKED THIS WAY WOULD BE *PASSED OVER* BY THE ANGEL OF DEATH AND GRANTED *LIFE*.

I CAN'T SLEEP... WHAT'S ALL THIS NOISE?

PHARAOH HEARD THE CRIES AND SCREAMS COMING FROM EVERY HOME IN EGYPT.

AAAAIEE!

SOB!

OUR SON... DEAD!

WHAT AM I GOING TO DO? I TOO, AM A FIRSTBORN! I COULD DIE ANY MINUTE!

I HATE TO ADMIT IT, THERE'S ONLY ONE PERSON TO TURN TO: MOSHE!

PREPARE MY CHARIOT. HURRY!

IN GOSHEN...

MOSHE! DO YOU HEAR ME? IT IS I, PHARAOH! GET UP AND LEAVE EGYPT NOW! ALL OF YOU!

MOSHE, SEE? I HAVE COME TO YOU AS YOU PREDICTED! **NOW LEAVE EGYPT!**

QUICKLY!

TAKE YOUR FAMILIES, YOUR ANIMALS, EVERYTHING... **JUST GO!**

AND PRAY FOR ME TOO!

SO HERE IT IS, THE MOMENT WE'VE WAITED AND PRAYED FOR. AFTER *210* YEARS OF BITTER SLAVERY, THE JEWISH PEOPLE ARE FINALLY FREE!

BUT NOT SO FAST, PHARAOH.

WHAT ARE YOU WAITING FOR? I WANT YOU TO LEAVE EGYPT. NOW! AT ONCE! THIS MINUTE! PRONTO!

WE SHALL NOT LEAVE LIKE THIEVES AT NIGHT...

WE SHALL LEAVE PROUDLY, IN THE LIGHT OF THE DAY, SO THAT ALL OF EGYPT WILL WITNESS THE GREAT WONDERS OF THE G-D OF ISRAEL!

IT'S ALMOST DAWN, MOSHE.

HOW ABOUT YOU AND YOUR PEOPLE GET AN EARLY START?!

NOT SO FAST.

JUST GO

HASTA LA VISTA! P.S. ARRIVEDERCI!

RUN... DON'T WALK!

DO SVIDANIYA

BONJOUR! ADIÓS

GOOD-BYE AND GOOD RIDDANCE!

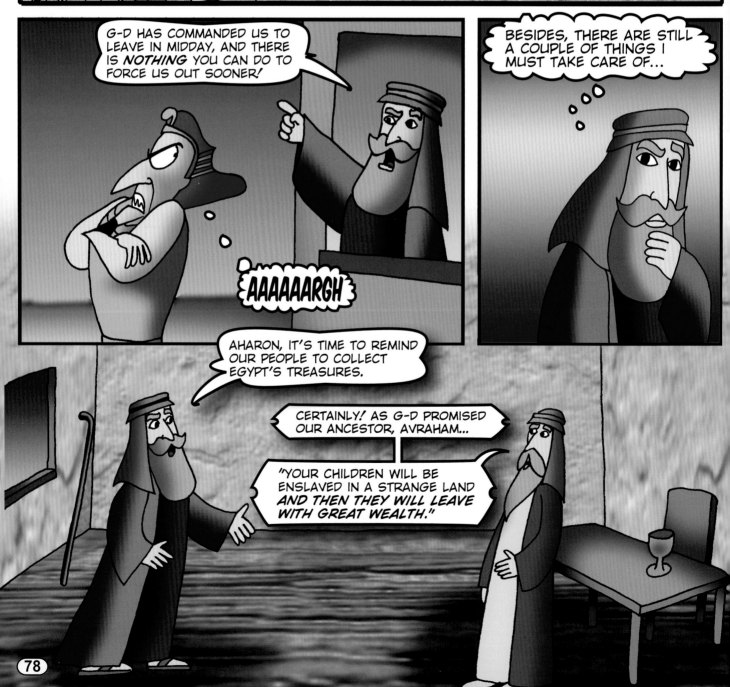

G-D HAS COMMANDED US TO LEAVE IN MIDDAY, AND THERE IS *NOTHING* YOU CAN DO TO FORCE US OUT SOONER!

BESIDES, THERE ARE STILL A COUPLE OF THINGS I MUST TAKE CARE OF...

AAAAAARGH

AHARON, IT'S TIME TO REMIND OUR PEOPLE TO COLLECT EGYPT'S TREASURES.

CERTAINLY! AS G-D PROMISED OUR ANCESTOR, AVRAHAM...

"YOUR CHILDREN WILL BE ENSLAVED IN A STRANGE LAND *AND THEN THEY WILL LEAVE WITH GREAT WEALTH.*"

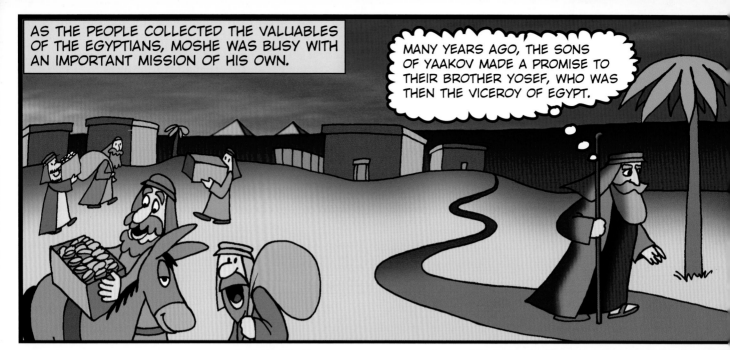

AS THE PEOPLE COLLECTED THE VALUABLES OF THE EGYPTIANS, MOSHE WAS BUSY WITH AN IMPORTANT MISSION OF HIS OWN.

MANY YEARS AGO, THE SONS OF YAAKOV MADE A PROMISE TO THEIR BROTHER YOSEF, WHO WAS THEN THE VICEROY OF EGYPT.

THIS PROMISE, BINDING ON THE JEWISH PEOPLE, WAS THAT WHEN THE TIME CAME FOR US TO LEAVE EGYPT, WE WOULD TAKE YOSEF'S BONES WITH US.

BUT WHERE IN ALL OF EGYPT COULD THEY BE?!

AS THE HOUR OF DEPARTURE DREW NEAR, MOSHE HAD SEARCHED ALL OVER BUT STILL HAD NOT FOUND YOSEF'S COFFIN.

NO DOUBT THE EGYPTIANS HAVE HIDDEN IT WELL, KNOWING THAT WE CANNOT LEAVE EGYPT WITHOUT IT.

AH! I KNOW! I'LL ASK SERACH, THE GRANDDAUGHTER OF YAAKOV. AS THE ONLY SURVIVING CHILD OF ASHER, YOSEF'S BROTHER, SHE MUST KNOW WHERE HER FAMOUS UNCLE IS BURIED.

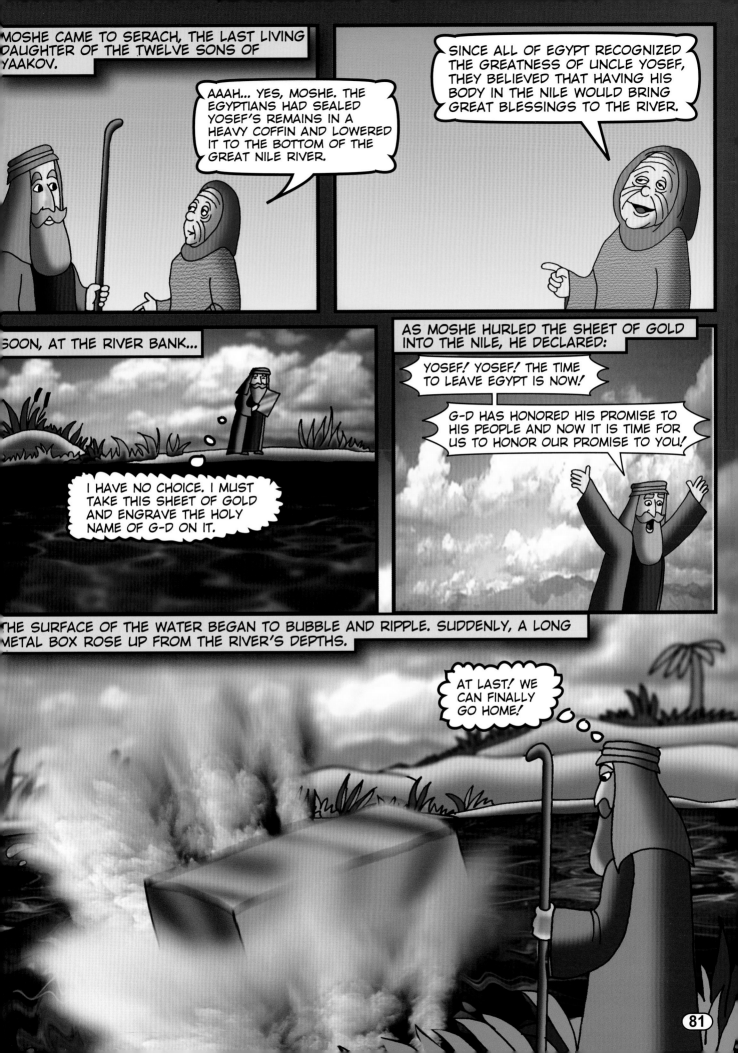

WITH THE EGYPTIANS PUSHING THE JEWISH PEOPLE TO LEAVE THE COUNTRY, THERE WAS NO TIME TO PROPERLY PREPARE FOOD FOR THE JOURNEY INTO THE WILDERNESS.

THEY HURRIEDLY LEFT WITH THE DOUGH STILL FRESH IN THEIR KNEADING BOWLS, AND BAGS OF MATZAH CARRIED UPON THEIR SHOULDERS.

AND SO, OVER 3,000 YEARS AGO, 600,000 MEN, ALONG WITH MILLIONS OF WOMEN AND CHILDREN, MARCHED **OUT OF EGYPT!**

NOT A DOG BARKED AS THEY LEFT THE LAND OF THEIR SLAVERY WITH THEIR HEARTS FULL OF JOY, HEADS HELD HIGH, AND SONGS OF PRAISE ON THEIR LIPS.

Insights

THROUGHOUT THE AGES, JEWS WORLDWIDE EAT MATZAH ON THE HOLIDAY OF PASSOVER.

THIS TRADITIONAL FOOD, WHICH THE JEWISH PEOPLE TOOK WITH THEM AS THEY TRAVELED TO FREEDOM, IS AN ETERNAL REMINDER OF THE HURRIED WAY THAT THEY LEFT EGYPT.

AS THE JEWS JOURNEYED THROUGH THE DESERT, G-D LOVINGLY PROVIDED THEM MIRACULOUS PROTECTION:

DURING THE DAY, A HUGE PILLAR OF CLOUD SHOWED THEM THE WAY AND PROTECTED THEM FROM THE HEAT OF THE BLAZING DESERT SUN...

AND AS NIGHT FELL, A SPECTACULAR PILLAR OF FIRE APPEARED TO LIGHT THEIR PATH, WHILE SHIELDING THEM FROM WILD BEASTS AND THE CHILLING COLD OF THE DESERT NIGHT.

BUT BACK IN EGYPT, A FUMING PHARAOH BROODS UPON HIS THRONE.

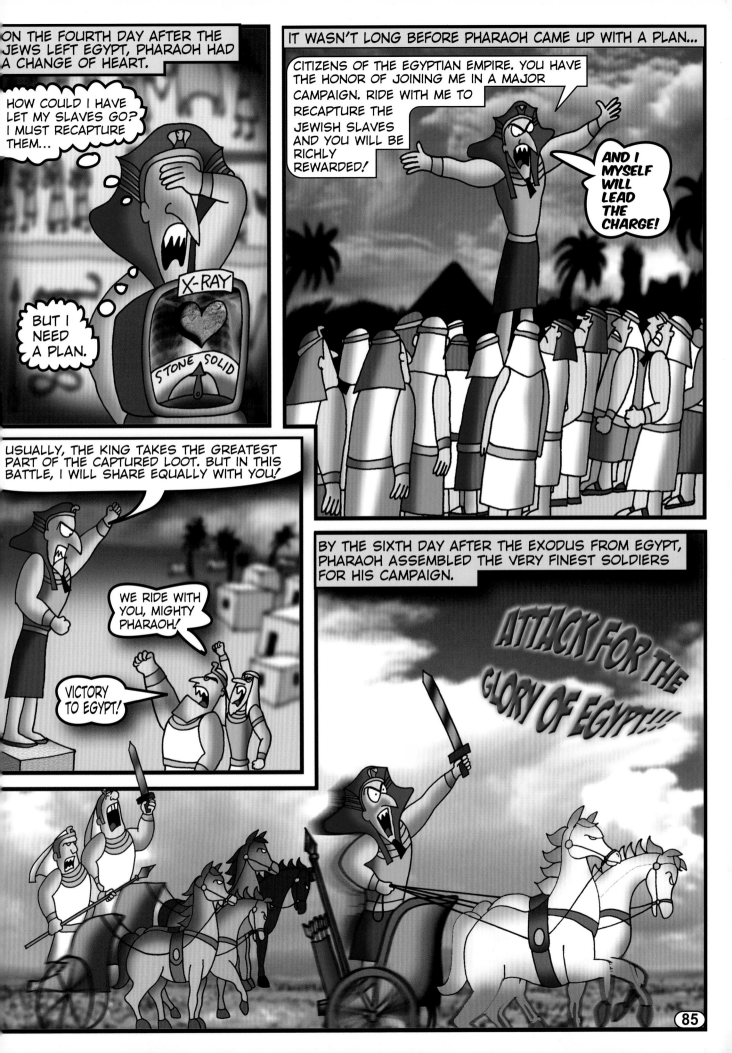

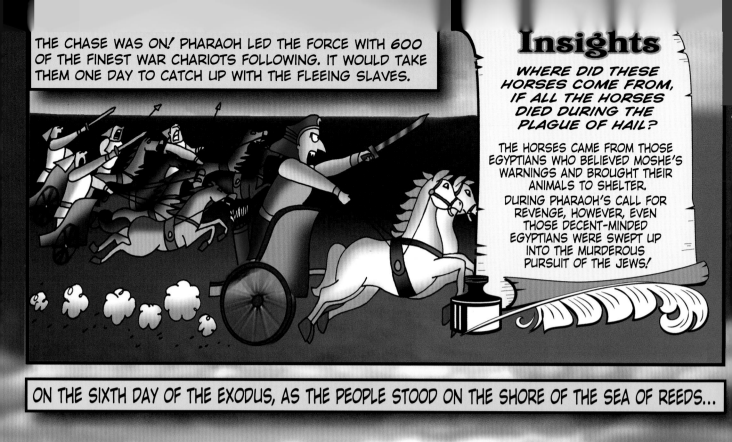

THE CHASE WAS ON! PHARAOH LED THE FORCE WITH 600 OF THE FINEST WAR CHARIOTS FOLLOWING. IT WOULD TAKE THEM ONE DAY TO CATCH UP WITH THE FLEEING SLAVES.

Insights

WHERE DID THESE HORSES COME FROM, IF ALL THE HORSES DIED DURING THE PLAGUE OF HAIL?

THE HORSES CAME FROM THOSE EGYPTIANS WHO BELIEVED MOSHE'S WARNINGS AND BROUGHT THEIR ANIMALS TO SHELTER. DURING PHARAOH'S CALL FOR REVENGE, HOWEVER, EVEN THOSE DECENT-MINDED EGYPTIANS WERE SWEPT UP INTO THE MURDEROUS PURSUIT OF THE JEWS!

ON THE SIXTH DAY OF THE EXODUS, AS THE PEOPLE STOOD ON THE SHORE OF THE SEA OF REEDS...

LOOK! THE EGYPTIAN ARMY!

AAAAIEEEEEE!

LED BY PHARAOH HIMSELF!

WE'RE TRAPPED!

LET'S RUN FOR OUR LIVES!

RUN?! RUN WHERE? INTO THE SEA?

MOSHE THEN LIFTED HIS STAFF TO THE SKY, AND A TREMENDOUS WIND FROM THE EAST BEGAN TO BLOW.

IT'S UNBELIEVABLE!

LOOK!

ANOTHER MIRACLE!

AS THE WIND BLEW, THE PILLARS OF CLOUD AND FIRE MOVED TO THE BACK OF THE JEWISH CAMP, BLOCKING THE ADVANCE OF THE EGYPTIANS AND PROTECTING THE JEWS.

WHAT'S GOING ON?

IS THIS SOME KIND OF MAGIC?

WE CAN GO NO FURTHER!

CHARIOTS, HALT!

THE CLOUD PILLAR THREW THE APPROACHING EGYPTIANS INTO TOTAL DARKNESS...

PHARAOH! HELP!

THE HORSES ARE PANICKING!

DON'T YOU CALL ME A HORSE!

STOP!

HALT!

MEANWHILE, IN THE JEWISH CAMP...

PEOPLE OF ISRAEL, PREPARE TO MOVE ON!

MOVE ON?!

WHERE? INTO THE SEA?

SUDDENLY, NACHSHON, SON OF AMINADAV, AND PRINCE OF THE TRIBE OF YEHUDAH, LEAPED INTO THE STORMY WAVES.

SEVERAL OF NACHSHON'S TRIBE FOLLOWED HIM, AS DID MANY OTHERS.

HELP... SAVE US!

GURGLE, GURGLE...

G-D THEN INSTRUCTED MOSHE TO RAISE HIS HANDS TOWARDS THE SEA AND SAY...

IN THE NAME OF G-D, I COMMAND YOU TO PART YOUR WATERS!

OPEN A PATH SO THAT THE JEWISH PEOPLE MAY PASS SAFELY!

WITH AN EARTH-SHATTERING SOUND, THE SEA OBEYED MOSHE'S COMMAND, SPREADING ITSELF APART UNTIL THE SEA FLOOR WAS EXPOSED.

ANOTHER THUNDEROUS CRASH WAS HEARD AS THE WATERS SHOT UP INTO THE SKY, FORMING TWO ENORMOUS SOLID WALLS.

THE FIRST BRAVE JEWS WHO HAD LEAPED INTO THE WAVES WERE NOW SAVED FROM DROWNING WHEN THE SEA PARTED.

GO ON. GO AHEAD. IT'S ALL RIGHT...

I'LL BE RIGHT BEHIND YOU... *HURRY NOW!*

THE FIERCE WIND CONTINUED TO BLOW AS THE JEWS WALKED ONTO THE DRY SEA LAND.

AS THEY WALKED FURTHER, THE SEA KEPT OPENING BEFORE THEM.

MOSHE STOOD AT THE ENTRANCE TO THE SEA AND WAITED UNTIL THE VERY LAST JEWS PASSED THROUGH.

WITH A THUNDEROUS CRASH, THE WATERS, WHICH PARTED FOR THE JEWISH PEOPLE, CAME CRASHING DOWN UPON PHARAOH'S ARMY, HURLING THEM DOWN TO THE BOTTOM OF THE SEA!

Insights

PHARAOH'S ADVENTURES

ACCORDING TO SOME SCHOLARS, PHARAOH DID NOT DROWN; HE SURVIVED TO BECOME KING OF ANCIENT NINVEH!

HE RULED THERE WHEN PROPHET YONAH ARRIVED TO URGE THE PEOPLE OF NINVEH TO REPENT. PHARAOH LED HIS PEOPLE IN PUTTING A QUICK END TO THEIR EVIL WAYS.

INDEED, PHARAOH OF EGYPT HAD FINALLY LEARNED HIS LESSON!

INSPIRED BY THE MIRACLES AT SEA, MOSHE COMPOSED A BEAUTIFUL **SHIRAH** (SONG). THE ENTIRE NATION BURST INTO SONG!

EVEN LITTLE BABIES JOINED IN!

LED BY MIRIAM, THE WOMEN TOOK UP MUSICAL INSTRUMENTS AND DANCED AS THEY SANG.

ON THE SIXTH DAY OF THE HEBREW MONTH OF SIVAN, MORE THAN FORTY DAYS AFTER THE MIRACULOUS SPLITTING OF THE SEA, THE JEWISH NATION CAME TO MOUNT SINAI AND RECEIVED THE TORAH. THE BLAST OF THE SHOFAR SOUNDED AND PIERCING THUNDER CAUSED THE EARTH TO TREMBLE!

THEY HAD RISEN FROM BEING THE LOWEST OF SLAVES TO TAKE ON THEIR SPECIAL DESTINY AS SERVANTS OF G-D, AND AS A LIGHT UNTO THE NATIONS OF THE WORLD!

Out of Egypt

An Illustrated Adaptation of the Book of Exodus

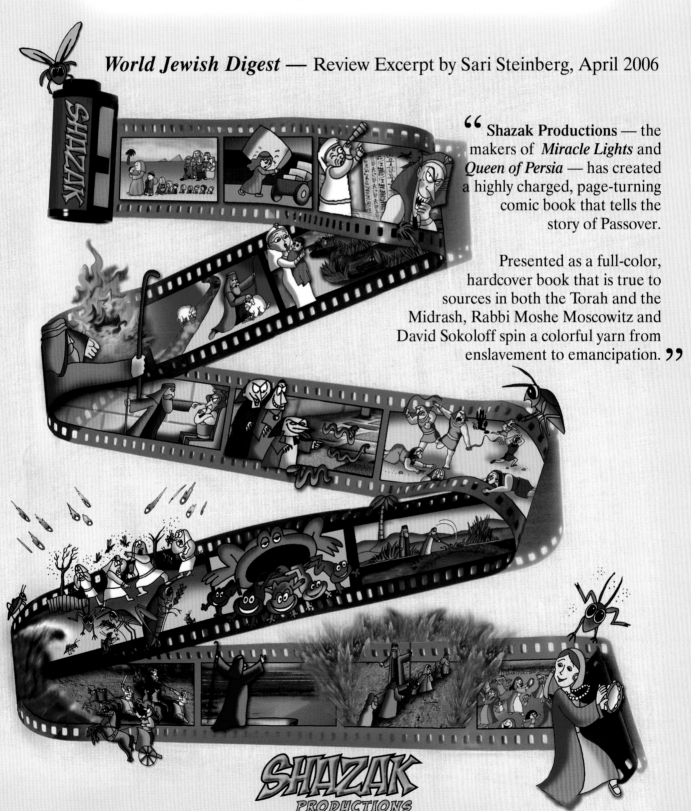

World Jewish Digest — Review Excerpt by Sari Steinberg, April 2006

" **Shazak Productions** — the makers of *Miracle Lights* and *Queen of Persia* — has created a highly charged, page-turning comic book that tells the story of Passover.

Presented as a full-color, hardcover book that is true to sources in both the Torah and the Midrash, Rabbi Moshe Moscowitz and David Sokoloff spin a colorful yarn from enslavement to emancipation. "

SHAZAK PRODUCTIONS

Test your **Out of Egypt** knowledge with **Quizzer**! For maximum enjoyment and plenty of laughs try **Quizzer** with a friend.

WHERE IS THE ANSWER-KEY?

> I MUST FIND OUT THE ANSWER! MAYBE THIS WILL WORK!

There is no answer-key!

If you're having a tough time, not even magic will help!

What's the solution?
It's time to read **Out of Egypt** again!

BUNGEE JUMPING TODAY 1-5 PM

ENJOY!!

QUIZZER

Pharaoh and his advisors were worried about the...

And on today's list of things to worry about...

1. Jewish-Population-Explosion.

2. Nile-River-Pollution-Smell.

3. What-Color-To-Paint-The-Throne-Dillema.

4. Pyramid-Mummy-Overcrowding-Problem.

AAARGH!

Such aggravation!

How did Pharaoh make the Jews' lives totally miserable?

More junk mail?

1. He made them slaves.

2. He outlawed all food that start with the letter **K** - no more **K**nishes, **K**ugel, **K**ishke, **K**replach, or **K**naidlach!

3. Any Jew caught speaking Yiddish would be severely punished.

4. He drafted them into the rough and tough Egyptian army.

WORSE...

Another decree from Pharaoh!

As a result of Pharaoh trying to cut down on the Jewish birthrate...

I can no longer count my kids.

Why not?

I've run out of fingers and toes!

1. fewer Jewish babies were born.

2. the Jewish mothers got a lot more sleep.

3. all "Babies 'R Us" stores went bankrupt.

4. the plan backfired and more Jewish babies were born than ever before!

QUIZZER

What was Pharaoh's command to the Jewish midwives, Shifrah and Puah?

1. Wash all the royal laundry in the palace three times a day.

2. Drown all newborn baby boys.

3. Kill all newborn baby boys.

4. Serve non-Kosher food to the mothers who gave birth.

...and do it NOW!

NEVER!!

What bad news did the stargazer tell Pharaoh?

Oh, no! I see blood everywhere!

1. A huge comet was heading straight for his palace!

2. A boy will be born who will lead the Jews to freedom.

3. Pharaoh will come down with a terrible case of chickenpox.

4. All turkeys were heading south for the winter.
   (Too bad for Pharaoh. He loved turkey!)

You fool! You're looking into a ketchup bottle!

Hey! I saw him first!

Yuk! Let go of me, you crawling handbag!

Who found the baby in the Nile River?

1. His brother, Aharon (some Rabbis say that it was his sister, Miriam).

2. Pharaoh's daughter.

3. An old Egyptian fisherman.

4. Good old Harry, the famous deep sea diver from the Bronx.

As a young man in the palace, it upset Moshe to see a Jew...

1. eating non-Kosher food.

2. wrestling with an Egyptian.

3. being beaten by an Egyptian slave driver.

4. being beaten by an Egyptian in an exciting game of chess.

I can't believe what I see... and it's ruining my appetite!

YIPPEE!

If that troublemaker hadn't butted in, I would've broken your nose!

And I'd still be better looking than you!

Who broke up the fight between the two Jews, Datan and Aviram?

1. Saddam Haddam and Abdullah Shmabdullah, two of the strongest Egyptian slave drivers.

2. Mrs. Datan and Mrs. Aviram. (Boy, were they angry!)

3. Moshe, the prince.

4. Aharon, the peacemaker.

Why did Moshe flee Egypt to go to Midyan?

1. There was a terrible hunger in Egypt.

2. He was tired of the hustle-bustle of Egypt and wanted to take it easy as a shepherd in Midyan.

3. He was afraid Pharaoh would sentence him to death for killing the Egyptian.

4. He received a Divine command at the burning bush.

Last camel leaving for Midyan! All aboard!

What did Moshe do in Midyan?

1. He married and settled down to a quiet life as a shepherd.

2. He led the Midyanites to freedom.

3. He taught the Midyanites how to build pyramids.

4. He lived in a cave and studied the Torah in secret.

YOU ARE NOW ENTERING MIDYAN

Land of wells, sheep, and Yitro's daughters.

At the Burning Bush, G-d told Moshe...

1. it's about time to find a better paying job.

2. where his lost sheep was hiding.

3. to take his family and move to the holy land of Canaan.

4. to go back to Egypt and lead his people out of slavery.

MOSHE! MOSHE!

Please excuse me, my little one. I must take this call.

QUIZZER

Did you see that third miracle last night?

Moshe was to demonstrate three miraculous signs to the Jews in Egypt. Which one was **not** one of them?

1. His hand turned white.

2. His staff became a snake.

3. His speech problem was cured.

4. The water turned into blood.

After Moshe told him to free the slaves, what new cruelty did Pharaoh force on the Jews?

1. He took away their cell phones.

2. He forced them to watch his terribly boring home videos.

3. He ordered them to gather their own straw to make bricks.

4. He ordered them to gather their own bricks to make straw.

Hey, Pharaoh! You can't be as mean and rotten as you seem!

How dare you say that?! Guards, take him away!

Something fishy is going on here!

Why did the fish in the Nile River die?

1. The river dried up.

2. The Egyptians were throwing too much garbage in the river.

3. The water of the river turned into blood.

4. There was a massive invasion of crocodiles (some scholars say that it was alligators).

During **The-Plague-of-Blood**, the only way the Egyptians were able to get water, was if they...

1. bought it from the Jews.

2. bought bottled spring water.

3. prayed that it would not turn to blood.

4. installed a very expensive filter in their sinks.

Let's see what happens if I combine these two.

QUIZZER

During which plague were creatures hopping into flaming ovens?

1. The-Plague-of-Creatures-Hopping-into-Flaming-Ovens.

2. The-Plague-of-Grasshoppers.

3. The-Plague-of-Darkness (the creatures were looking for a well lighted place).

4. The-Plague-of-Frogs.

Enough is enough! We're moving to Arizona!

Why couldn't the Egyptian magicians duplicate the creation of lice?

Hey Pharaoh! Watch me pull a rabbit out of my hat!

1. Simple... it is a well-known fact that ancient Egyptians were allergic to lice.

2. Lice are just too small to create by use of magic.

3. Egyptians can't stand the sight of bugs.

4. They lost their magical powers during The-Plague-of-Frogs.

I'm surrounded by ninkumpoops!

Which plague came after The-Plague-of-Lice?

What's going on here? Did someone sign me up for the Plague-of-the-Month-Club?!

1. The-Plague-After-the-Plague-of-Lice-Plague.

2. The-Plague-of-Toothaches-and-Bad-Breath.

3. The-Plague-of-Wild-Animals.

4. The-Plague-of-Hail.

During The-Plague-of-Wild-Animals...

1. Egypt was flooded with tourists who came to watch this wild plague.

2. Pharaoh opened a zoo and forced the Jews to sell highly overpriced tickets.

3. the wild animals helped the Jews with their harsh labor.

4. the beasts tore apart trees, crops and gardens.

WELCOME TO EGYPT ZOO OF THE MIDEAST

103

Which Egyptian animals survived during The-Plague-of-Cattle-Disease?
Those animals...

Sounds Psych-cow-somatic to me.

My head is spinnin'...

1. that were Kosher.

2. that had been vaccinated with their Plague Shots.

3. that had medical insurance.

4. that belonged to the Jewish people.

Blood, frogs, lice, beasts, cattle plague... What's next?

To start the sixth plague, Moshe threw...

1. soot into the air - which brought about **The-Plague-of-Blisters**.

2. a baseball around - just to relax a bit.

3. giant rocks at the mean Egyptian taskmasters.

4. none of the above.

Here's a hint....
How's your supply of skin cream?

After witnessing The-Plague-of-Hail, Pharaoh finally admitted that...

It's about time!

1. he has a terrible case of bad breath.

2. he used to cheat on his high-school spelling tests.

3. his people are wicked.

4. both Pharaoh and his people are wicked.

And today's weather report:

Total darkness, followed by 100% pitch-black darkness...

COULD SOMEONE PLEASE TURN ON THE LIGHTS!

Why couldn't the Egyptians see? Because...

1. of **The Plague of Broken Glasses**.

2. of **The-Plague-of-Darkness**.

3. their eyes were closed (they could not bear to see any more destruction).

4. they were blinded by the burning desert sun.

QUIZZER

Get a look at my giraffe hand-shadow!

What did many Jews do during "The Plague of Darkness?"

1. They made funny faces at the Egyptians.

2. They made a quick escape from Egypt.

3. They entered the Egyptians homes and saw where the valuables were hidden.

4. They lit candles so that they could continue learning Torah.

Wise advisors! What do you counsel as the fateful hour approaches?

At exactly midnight, the day before the exodus, the...

Let's break all the clocks so midnight never comes!

1. firstborn cattle collapsed due to "The Midnight Cattle Disease".

2. firstborn Jews went out of Egypt.

3. firstborn Egyptians died.

4. The price of firstborn camels skyrocketed.

Come on already. Go, go, get out! You can even borrow my luggage...

JUST GO!

During "The Plague of the Firstborn," Pharaoh begged Moshe to leave Egypt. What did Moshe answer?

1. That's wonderful! We're leaving right now!

2. We'll wait till the daytime so all can witness the grand exodus.

3. Absolutely nothing; Moshe was left speechless.

4. How do you expect my people to survive in the hot, bitter desert?

What did G-d command the Jews to tie to their bedposts?

1. Their blankets; due to "The Plague of the Wind," which kept blowing them away.

2. A red heifer (a young cow).

3. Their shoelaces; so the Egyptians wouldn't steal them - (shoes are very important in the hot desert).

4. A lamb.

BUNGEE JUMPING TODAY 1-5 PM

QUIZZER

The Jews were commanded to eat the Passover Sacrifice with...

1. a fork in the left hand and a knife in the right.

2. Egyptian chopsticks (Chinese chopsticks weren't invented yet).

3. their shoes on their feet, staffs in their hands; ready to make a quick exit out of Egypt.

4. their hats on their heads, running shoes on their feet and passports in their hands.

DRIVE-THRU

I'll have the roast lamb combo.

BOING!
BOING!
BOING!
BOING
SWISS ARMY PACK

Your backpack's gone haywire!

What were the Jewish people carrying on their knapsacks as they left Egypt?

1. Bottled water and plenty of mosquito repellant.

2. Matzahs.

3. Souvenirs from the Egyptian pyramids.

4. Super high protein energy bars.

Moshe had to take Yosef's coffin out of Egypt, but...

1. it was much too heavy.

2. it was in the Egyptian Historical Museum.

3. he couldn't find it.

4. it was severely damaged during **The-Ten-Plagues**.

What's Moshe looking for?

A coffin.

Really? He looks healthy to me.

I don't care what he's wearing, son. There's no room in the wagon.

What did the dogs do as the Jewish people left Egypt?

1. They barked frantically.

2. They cheered wildly.

3. They stood by quietly.

4. They nibbled on matzah crumbs that fell from the Jews' backpacks.

While the Jews were traveling through the desert, they were led by...

1. a police escort by day and the National Guard by night.

2. the very latest GPS navigation system (invented by the ancient Egyptians).

3. a cloud by day and a fire by night.

4. a compass by day and the North Star at night.

Watch where you're going, Sarah!

Come on in, everyone... The water's perfect!

Nachshon jumped into the sea and...

1. gave the entire Jewish people swimming lessons so they could make a super-swift-swim-escape.

2. caught the first gefilte fish.

3. was never seen again.

4. walked through the water until it reached his neck and then the sea split.

What happened to the Jews when they walked through the sea?

1. They got wet.

2. The ground dried up and G-d provided food and water for them.

3. Their shoes got stuck in the mud.

4. Kosher fish jumped into their baskets.

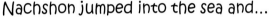

Now that's what I call special effects!

Hello. Motor Club? Can you get here before the sea comes crashing down on my head?

What two things did NOT happen to the Egyptians when they entered the sea?

1. They were bitten by sharks.

2. The walls of water came crashing upon their heads.

3. Their horses swam across the seas as their riders sank to the bottom.

4. Pharaoh's entire army drowned.

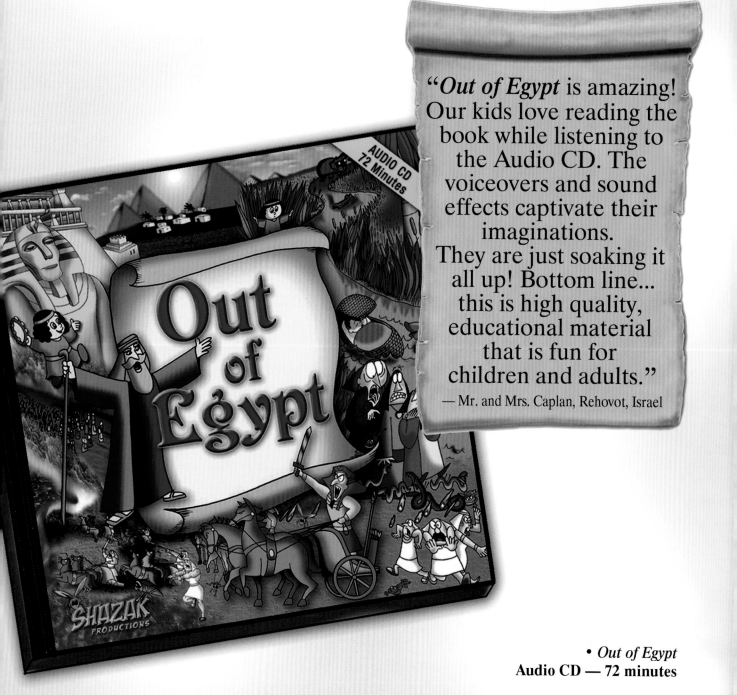

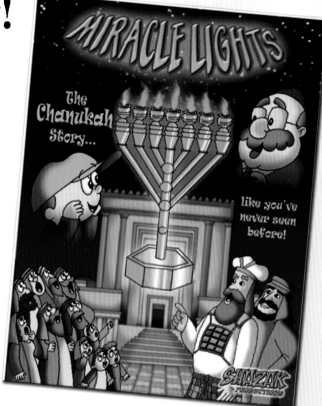

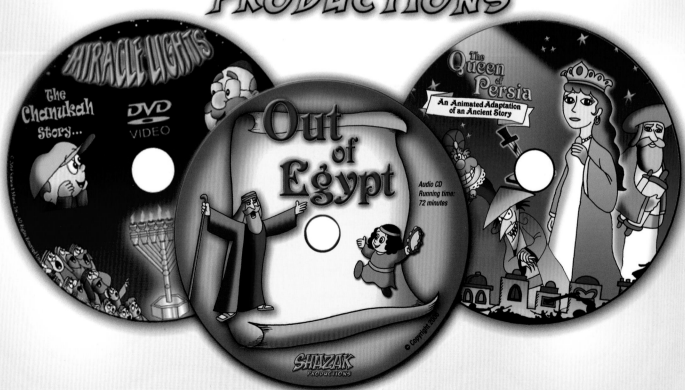